PAPERCUTZ™

MORE GREAT GRAPHIC NOVEL SERIES AVAILABLE FROM
PAPERCUTZ™

THE SMURFS #21

BRINA THE CAT #1

CAT & CAT #1

THE SISTERS #1

ATTACK OF THE STUFF

ASTERIX #1

SCHOOL FOR EXTRATERRESTRIAL GIRLS #1

GERONIMO STILTON REPORTER #1

THE MYTHICS #1

GUMBY #1

MELOWY #1

BLUEBEARD

THE RED SHOES

THE LITTLE MERMAID

FUZZY BASEBALL #1

HOTEL TRANSYLVANIA #1

THE LOUD HOUSE #1

MANOSAURS #1

THE ONLY LIVING BOY #5

THE ONLY LIVING GIRL #1

papercutz.com
Also available where ebooks are sold.

The Sisters

"5. M.Y.O.B."

Story
Cazenove & William
Art and colors
William

PAPERCUT**Z**
New York

Thank you to Olivier and Christopher, as well as The Bamboo Team. It's always a pleasure to work with you on this series.
To all the crazy Aveyron walkers and runners. The Portnawak Run is an allusion to the Nawak Run obstacle course in Millau.

Wendy: Maureen, are you ready for some new adventures¿
Maureen: Yup! And I'm going to blow you away, because I'm besters·at running than you.
Wendy: Whatevs! I'm going to teach you a lesson, shrimp!
Wendy: By the way, Daddy and Uncle Tof, did you have to place that little brat on my back at the prom¿
Maureen: Umm, hmm, oh, looky here, you're a little brat, too... Plus, Daddy wanted me to espy on the sly, so there!
Wendy: And you, of course, didn't need to hear anything else, since it was about delving into my private life, right¿
Maureen: Well, somebody has to stop you from getting into mischief, whether you like it or not, wouldn't you say¿
Wendy: "Mischief"¿ o_o
Maureen: Don't act like you're igno-rancing... That thing you and Mason do with your mouths! Wellll, yuck, yuck, just thinking about it, makes me break out in heebie-jeebies all over.
Wendy: Pff, pathetic!
Maureen: Huh¿ What pandemic¿

The Sisters #5 "M.Y.O.B."
Les Sisters [The Sisters] by Cazenove and William
Originally published in French as *Les Sisters tome 9 "Toujours Dans les Pattes!"* and *Les Sisters tome 10 "Survitaminées!"*
© 2014, 2015, 2019 Bamboo Édition
Sisters, characters and related indicia are copyright, trademark and exclusive license of Bamboo Edition.
English translation and all other editorial material © 2019 by Papercutz.
All rights reserved.

Story by Cazenove and William
Art and color by William
Cover by William
Translation by Nanette McGuinness
Lettering by Wilson Ramos Jr.
Special Thanks to Catherine Loiselet

Papercutz books may be purchased for business or promotional use. For information on bulk purchases please contact Macmillan Corporate and Premium Sales Department at (800) 221-7945 x5442

Production – Mark McNabb
Editor – Jeff Whitman
Editorial Intern – Izzy Boyce-Blanchard
Editor-in-Chief
Jim Salicrup

PB ISBN: 978-1-54580-341-7
HC ISBN: 978-1-54580-340-0

Printed in India
October 2020

Distributed by Macmillan
Second Papercutz Printing

HA HA! THAT'S YOUR SISTER AT TOP SPEED.

YES, A REAL LI'L MONKEY!

SHE'D DO A HIGH ROPES COURSE ALL DAY LONG, IF SHE COULD, YOU KNOW.

I'M THE BEST CLIMBSINGER IN THE WOOORLD!

YEEHAAH!

MY TURN ON THE ZIPZAPLINE!

SUPER SISTEEEEER!

YOU COULD TELL HER THAT A PLATE OF SPINACH WAS WAITING ON THE OTHER SIDE AND SHE'D STILL GO ANYWAY.

LOL

EVEN THOUGH SHE HATES SPINACH!

HEY, THAT GIVES ME AN IDEA...

WITH A ZIP LINE TO THE BATHTUB, YOU WON'T GRIPE ABOUT TAKING A SHOWER ANYMORE, MAUREEN!

HUMPF!

IF THIS WORKS, I CAN INSTALL ONE FOR YOU THAT GOES FROM YOUR BEDROOM WINDOW TO SCHOOL...

CAZENOVE & WILLIAM

YAAAWN!

OKAY, WELL, I'M GOING TO SLEEP.

AHEM, I'M SAYING THAT I'M GOING TO SLEEP...

...I'M NOT GOING TO WAIT, BY THE WAY...I'M GOING TO SLEEP...

I'M GOING RIGHT NOW...

I'M GOING TO SLEEP!

OKAY!

I COULD'VE TOLD YOU IT WAS A BAD IDEA TO LET HER WATCH THAT NEWS REPORT ABOUT THE QUEEN OF ENGLAND.

FASTER, FASTER...

MY ROYAL SLEEP WON'T WAIT!

CAZENOVE & WILLIAM

LOOK OUT, SAMMIE!

I KNOW, I KNOW. YOU'RE GOING TO ASK ME WHY SISTER'S CLIMBING TREES.

BINGO!

ACTUALLY, WE'RE PLAYING *TWENTY QUESTIONS*. I GIVE HER A PENALTY FOR EVERY WRONG ANSWER...

SHE CLIMBS THE TREE AND COMES BACK DOWN OVER BY THE TRASH CANS...

...HOPS THROUGH THE MUD LIKE A BUNNY AND SOMERSAULTS BACK HERE.

IS THAT ALL? WOW! YOUR PENALTIES ARE CHALLENGING!

"YOU DON'T GO EASY ON HER. POOR MAUREEN!"

≈HUFF≈
≈PUFF≈

≈HUMPH≈

COME ON! ANOTHER QUESTION, WENDY. I'M SUPER-DUPER READY!

OKAY, WHAT COLOR IS THE SEA?

I KNOW! PISTACHIO GREEN AND NEON PINK!

BZZZT!

YYYYAAAAAYYYY!

LOL!

I LOST AGAINNNN...

WELL, YEAH. MY SISTER LOVES THE PENALTIES!

CAZENOVE & WILLIAM

WENDY, WENDY, I'M GOING TO SHOW YOU A MINDHOBGOBBLING MAGIC TRICK.

LULU TAUGHT IT TO ME.

AH, YUP. TOTALLY.

WHAT'RE YOU RUMMAGING AROUND FOR THERE?

WELLLL, I NEED A BOOK... A SQUARE ONE... YOU KNOW?!

WELL, HECK.

AW, RATS. I SPOTTED ONE LIKE THAT HERE YESTERDAY.

REALLY, I WASN'T HALLUCINACHING!

GET A MAGAZINE OR A CALENDAR. OR MOM'S NOVEL.

NO, NO, NO, IT WON'T WORK WITH THOSE!

LULU TOLD ME I HAD TO HAVE A SQUAAAAARE BOOK... AND I DON'T HAVE OOOOOONNNNNE...

DON'T CRY, MAUREEN. YOU CAN DO YOUR TRICK WITH MY PRIVATE DIARY IF YOU'D LIKE. WHAT DO YOU SAY ABOUT THAT?

SNIFF! AT LEAST IT'S SQUARE-ISH, RIGHT?

WELL, IN THAT CASE, CONCENTRATE REALLY HARD BECAUSE IT'S GOING TO GO AWAY VERY, VERY QUICKLY...

MM-HMM...

IT'S MINDHOBGOBBLING HOW I FELL FOR IT...

CAZENOVE & WILLIAM

JUNGLE GHIRL OF THE SAVAAAANNAH!

CABLAM

SCREEECH

?!

WAAAAH!

CHARLIE IS BROKENNNN... ≥BOOO-HOOOOOO!≥...

MY CON-CENTRATION IS BROKEN TOO. ≥HUMPH.≥

WELL, GIVE HIM TO ME. I'LL SORT HIM OUT. JUST YOU WAIT AND SEE.

BUT LOOK. HIS LEG IS COMPLETELY TORN OFF.

FIRST, A MASK TO PUT HIM TO SLEEP...

THAT'S SO HE WON'T SUFFER?!

EXACTLY!

AND A NEEDLE AND SOME THREAD. HE'LL GET BACK HIS LITTLE PAW.

AND THAT WON'T HURT HIM?

TRUST "DOCTOR WENDY."

AND THERE YOU GO...THE OPERATION WAS A SUCCESS.

≥GAAH!≥ YOU'RE SO AMAZING! LET'S ALL THREE OF US PLAY JUNGLE GIRL OF THE SAVANNAH.

≥ACK!≥ NO. THE MOST IDIOTIC GAME I KNOW.

UNLESS...

OOH, BOY...IT'S NICE AND CALM HERE, GIRLS...

SHHH... YOU MUSTN'T MAKE ANY NOISE. WENDY TOLD ME THAT CHARLIE HAS TO STAY QUIET FOR A WEEK TO RECOVER FROM HIS OPERATION.

DOCTOR WENDY IS SO BRILLIANT!

CAZENOVE & WILLIAM

THE SEA, THE SEA... THE SEEEEA!

⸗ARGGH!⸗ CALM DOWN ALREADY, MAUREEN, ⸗GRR!⸗...

QUIIICK!...I WANT TO GO SWIMMING RIGHT AWAAAAY!

TOOOOT TOOOOT

BEEEEP BEEEEP HONK

I KNOW MY SISTER BACKWARDS AND FORWARDS...

LET THE QUEEN OF THE OCEAN THROUGH! YEEHAW!

AND I KNOW THAT WHEN SHE'S GOING ALL OUT LIKE THIS...

FB

....IT'S BECAUSE THERE'S A WATERING HOLE NEARBY.

SPLISH SPLISH SPLISH

FLIPPER THE DOLPHIN: THAT'S ME!

IT WORKS WITH POOLS, TOO...

LAST ONE IN IS A ROTTEN EGG!

BOILING

WATER SLIDES...

HELLO... IT'S WATER, YOU KNOW!

DON'T MENTION WHEN IT RAINS!...

THREE! FOUR! GLUB

YUM!

YEP, MY SISTER AND WATER: A GREAT BIG LOVE AFFAIR, YOU KNOW?

CRAZY!

OOL

BUT EVERY NIGHT, IT'S A TOTAL PAIN TO MAKE HER TAKE A SHOWER...

NOOOO, NOT A SHOOOOWER...THEN I'LL BE ALL WET AFTERWARDS...

BOTTOM LINE, SOMETIMES I HAVE TROUBLE UNDERSTANDING MY SISTER...

SHOWERS

CAZENOVE & WILLIAM

HA HA! THAT'S YOUR SISTER AT TOP SPEED.

YES, A REAL LI'L MONKEY!

SHE'D DO A HIGH ROPES COURSE ALL DAY LONG, IF SHE COULD, YOU KNOW.

I'M THE BEST CLIMBSINGER IN THE WOOORLD!

YEEHAAH!

MY TURN ON THE ZIPZAPLINE!

SUPER SISTEEEER!

YOU COULD TELL HER THAT A PLATE OF SPINACH WAS WAITING ON THE OTHER SIDE AND SHE'D STILL GO ANYWAY.

LOL

EVEN THOUGH SHE HATES SPINACH!

HEY, THAT GIVES ME AN IDEA...

WITH A ZIP LINE TO THE BATHTUB, YOU WON'T GRIPE ABOUT TAKING A SHOWER ANYMORE, MAUREEN!

HUMPF!

IF THIS WORKS, I CAN INSTALL ONE FOR YOU THAT GOES FROM YOUR BEDROOM WINDOW TO SCHOOL...

CAZENOVE & WILLIAM

YAAAWN!

OKAY, WELL, I'M GOING TO SLEEP.

AHEM, I'M SAYING THAT I'M GOING TO SLEEP...

...I'M NOT GOING TO WAIT, BY THE WAY...I'M GOING TO SLEEP...

I'M GOING RIGHT NOW...

I'M GOING TO SLEEP!

OKAY!

I COULD'VE TOLD YOU IT WAS A BAD IDEA TO LET HER WATCH THAT NEWS REPORT ABOUT THE QUEEN OF ENGLAND.

FASTER, FASTER...

MY ROYAL SLEEP WON'T WAIT!

CAZENOVE & WILLIAM

THE PROBLEM WITH MAUREEN IS THAT WHEN SHE LIKES A GAME, SHE DOESN'T KNOW WHEN TO STOP...

TAG! YOU'RE IT!

AH, YOU GOT ME!

TAG! YOU'RE IT!

THIS GAME'S COOL!

WAP

SPRITZZ

TAG!

YOU'RE A PAIN, Y'KNOW?

WAP

TAG!

WAP

TAG! YOU'RE IT!

WAP

HONESTLY, THAT'S ENOUGH...

YOU'VE GOT A REAL PROBLEM... YOU DON'T KNOW WHEN TO STOP!

WHATEVS! PHOOEY...

THAT'S PUTTING IT MILDLY...

TAG!

SMAK

CAZENOVE & WILLIAM

13

SNOOPING AROUND IN MY ROOM AGAIN, EH?

I CAN'T BELIEVE THIS... DO I HAVE TO PUT A PADLOCK ON MY DOOR OR A DOBERMAN IN FRONT OF IT TO KEEP YOU FROM PROWLING AROUND HERE?

I...I DREW A REALLY PRETTY PICTURE AND I WANTED TO PUT IT ON YOUR PILLOW.

WELL, OKAY. I'M TOO STUPID. I CAN SEE YOU DON'T LIKE IT...

I WON'T BOTHER YOU ANYMORE.

BUT, BUT, BUT NO, IT'S REALLY CUTE. YOU'RE SO SWEET. I DIDN'T MEAN IT... I'M SORRY, REALLY SORRY, MAUREEN...

I'M REALLY TOUCHED, I SWEAR! THAT'S WONDERFUL. I'M SO STUPID...

THAT'S OKAY... NO BIG DEAL... I GET IT...

I'M SORRY, REALLY!

⩫PHEW!⩫...THAT WAS TOO CLOSE FOR COMFORT...

I NEED TO REMEMBER TO ALWAYS HAVE A DRAWING WITH ME, JUST IN CASE...

CAZENOVE & WILLIAM

14

CAZENOVE & WILLIAM

≈PHEW!≈...YOU'VE MADE A LOT OF PROGRESS AT DRAWING, WENDY. YOUR PORTRAITS TOTALLY LOOK REAL. THIS IS SO GREAT!

UH, UH THANKS...I PRACTICE BY DRAWING MY SISTER EVERY DAY.

I CAN TELL! THIS IS AWESOME!

HEY! WILL YOU DRAW MY PICTURE?

SURE! STAY RIGHT THERE.

INSPIRATION, CONCENTRATION.

HMMM

HMM HMM GRUMBLE

UH, SAMMIE... YOU WOULDN'T WANT TO RUN OR SKIP A BIT, WOULD YOU?

SAY WHAT?

I'M NOT USED TO DRAWING WITH A STATIONARY MODEL.

RIBBIT RIBBIT

CAZENOVE & WILLIAM

I'VE DRAWN WENDY'S ROOM REALLY WELL.

HIDING PLACYE

TAYBLE LAMPE

HIDING PLAYCE

WENDY'S BEDD

NIGHTSTEND

PRESSIR FORBIDDIN TOO YOU

HIDING PLAYCE

PIGSTY FOR CLEENINK UP

SECRET DRAWR

HIDING PLAYCE

EMURGENSY EGGSIT

HIDING PLAYCE

KLOZET

I'M GOING TO TELL YOU HOW TO SEARCH EVERYWHERE TO UNEARTH HER PRIVATE DIARY.

HOLD ON, MAUREEN. WHY ARE *YOU* ALWAYS THE COMMANDER?

WE'RE BRAVE, TOO, YOU KNOW?!

THERE'S NO REASON YOU SHOULD BE IN CHARGE EVERY TIME.

HEY, HEY, HEY! WHAT'RE YOU PESTS SCHEMING AGAIN IN MY ROOM?

WELL... ME...I...I

AND WE... G... R... I.... ⸓GASP⸓

⸓GULP!⸓

I... WE... I...

⸓GULP!⸓

UM

WE WERE LOOKING FOR HOW TO MAKE GUYS INVITE US TO THE PROM.

THAT'S ALL!

MAKE A GUY DANCE? ⸓PFFFT!⸓ GOOD LUCK GIRLS. THAT'S ALMOST MISSION IMPOSSIBLE...

GO ON AND DON'T MAKE A MESS, OKAY?

⸓PHEW!⸓... OKAY, OKAY, MAUREEN. YOU'RE THE BOSS!

YOU'RE THE BOSS FOR LIFE!

SO, I WAS TELLING YOU HOW TO SEARCH EVERYWHERE.

CAZENOVE & WILLIAM

FOR SEVERAL WEEKS, MAUREEN'S BEEN TAKING SWIMMING LESSONS...

THERE'S NOTHING BETTER FOR SELF-CONFIDENCE.

I'M SLINKLING. I'M GOING TO--≷GLUB BBLL BLL≶...

NOT AT ALL! YOU'RE STARTING TO BE ABLE TO FLOAT.

VERY GOOD. TRY TO COORDINATE YOUR ARMS AND LEGS...THAT'S IT!

YOU GOT IT! YOU'RE MAKING QUICK PROGRESS.

YOU SWIM LIKE A HIGH-QUALITY FISH.

HEE HEE!

AT THE BEACH...

YOU'LL BE ABLE TO PUT EVERYTHING YOU'VE LEARNED INTO PRACTICE, MAUREEN.

LOL. THE SANDY DOG PADDLER.

AND MOST OF ALL, YOU'RE GOING TO SWIM WITHOUT YOUR TUBE.

WHY'M I BEING PUNIIIISHED...I DIDN'T DO ANYTHING...I WANT MY ≷SHREEEEK!≶ TUBE.

WAAAHH

ANYHOW, WE'VE STILL GOT A WAYS TO GO FOR SELF-CONFIDENCE...

CAZENOVE & WILLIAM

AND AT SCHOOL, THE TEACHER ORGANIZED ALL OUR LESSONS AROUND *DANCE.*

AND IT WAS *SO* GREAT!

WOW!

YOU'RE SO LAME!

"IN FRENCH CLASS, WE HAD A DICTATION ABOUT *MODERN DANCE*...

.THEIR FEET FLUTTERED LIKE YOUNG BUTTERFLIES WITH CHROME WINGS...PERIOD!

CHROME, AS IN NICKEL-CHROME?

"...IN HISTORY, WE TALKED ABOUT THE MINUET...

TEACHER...

DID LOUIS XIV LIVE BELOW LOUIS XV?

...IN MATH, WE CALCULATED THE AREA OF A DANCE FLOOR...

I GOT 2 MILES. IS THAT TOO BIG?

WELL, NO. THAT'S BARELY THE SIZE OF MY ROOM.

"AND IN GEOGRAPHY, WE HAD TO FIND WHERE WORLD DANCES CAME FROM."

AND IN THE UNITED STATES?

COUNTRYYYY!

THE SAME IN P.E....

CLICK CLICK

NO WAYYY...YOU LEARNED DANCES IN P.E.? YOUR TEACHER'S FANTASTIC!

"OF COURSE NOT. WE TRIED TO GET OURSELVES A DANCING PARTNER FOR THE DANCE...

"...NOT EASY!"

CAZENOVE & WILLIAM

HEY, *TONY*...

DO YOU WANT TO BE MY KNIGHT FOR THE DANCE?

HUH? UH...

WHAT DO YOU MEAN BY, "UH?" YOU'VE ALREADY ASKED ANOTHER GIRL, MAYBE?

IN OTHER WORDS, MY SISTER MEANS NO MORE TO YOU THAN AN ALREADY-OPENED BAG OF PEANUTS? IS THAT IT?!

AND BESIDES, AS FAR AS I KNOW, SHE'S ALWAYS BEEN NICE TO YOU!

SHE DOESN'T DESERVE TO BE TREATED THAT WAY, DOES SHE, TONY?!

≋GULP!≋ YES, YES... UMM, I WAS GOING TO SAY, "YES, OF COURSE..."

HUH HUH

WE'LL DEFINITELY GO TO THE DANCE TOGETHER.

MY KNIGHT!

I'M SO HAPPY!

AND YOU'RE GOING TO INVITE ME TO THE PROM, AREN'T YOU, *MASON*?

AH, YES, UM, YES, I'M SO HAPPY!

HMM HMM

YAHOO!

CAZENOVE & WILLIAM

HEY, WENDY, AM I BOTHERING YOU?

NO, WHY?!

WHAT DOES *CALIFORKTINE* MEAN?

WELL, YOU KNOW HOW TO READ NOW. SO, YOU CAN GET THE DICTIONARY FROM DAD'S OFFICE AND LOOK IT UP.

AND BINGO! THANK YOU, DICTIONARY. WHAT A BRILLIANT IDEA.

≳MMMPH.≲ THIS BIGDIXTHINGIE...

THIS MILLAN MUST BE EXTRA MUSCLED.

NOT JUST TO TEACH MY SISTER...

BUT MOSTLY SO SHE'LL LEAVE ME ALONE...

OH, HEY. THIS DIXIE HAIRY IS TOTALLY USELESS.

WHAT DO YOU MEAN, TOTALLY USELESS?

WELL, THERE'S NOTHING IN IT.

NOTHING IN IT?

LOOK...IT DOESN'T EVEN HAVE "KALIFORKTANE!"

EVEN WORSE, IT ALSO DOESN'T HAVE, *CERRANNAID, SUPER KOOL,* OR *NLUV...*

...IT'S USELESS!

ACTUALLY, AN ENGLISH/MAUREEN DICTIONARY WOULD BE TERRIFIC.

CAZENOVE & WILLIAM

THERE'RE TIMES I'D LIKE TO BE ALONE A LITTLE.

≠SIGH≠

WHAT DO YOU SAY ABOUT HAVING A RACE, GIRLS? HARACE?

HARACE?

NOW?

WELL, YES! THE WEATHER'S GORGEOUS. MIGHT AS WELL TAKE ADVANTAGE OF IT. AND BESIDES, YOU'VE ALREADY SEEN THIS MOVIE A THOUSAND TIMES.

I'M IN!

COOL! PLUS, I LOVE RACES!

WOW! I'LL NEVER COME BACK IF YOU LEND ME YOUR SKATEBOARD!

YUP! AND I CAN TELL YOU'LL LIKE WHAT I'VE DONE WITH IT.

I'M GOING TO BEAT YOUR BUTT, MAUREEN.

YOU'LL HAVE TO CATCH ME FIRST.

READY... SET...

GO!

MOST OF ALL, GO. FOR TWO HOURS OF PEACE AND QUIET.

FULL SPEED...

WE ALWAYS DO THAT NOW. WE CALL IT THE "WRONG WAY AROUND RACE!" HA HA!

AND I'M THE WINNER!

I'LL HAVE TO THINK OF SOMETHING ELSE SO THAT I CAN FINALLY BE ALONE.

CAZENOVE & WILLIAM

HEEEEY, YOU'RE TAKING UP ALL THE ROOM! HAVE YOU GAINED WEIGHT OR *WHAT?!*

⋜PTOOEY!⋝ Y'SPITTIN' 'VERYWHERE!

THIS BATHROOM ISN'T BIG ENOUGH FOR THE TWO OF US!

YEAH, SO YOU AND YOUR JACKAL FACE SHOULD GO. HEH HEH HEH!

SPROTCH
SPROTCH

OH, COME ON! ARE YOU GIRLS CRAZY OR WHAT? CLEAN THIS UP RIGHT NOW!

AND THEN CLEAN YOURSELVES!

GRUMBLL...

CLUP

THIS BATHTUB ISN'T BIG ENOUGH FOR THE TWO OF US!

YEAH, HA HA HA! TAKE THAT, YOU EYESORE!

SPOOSH

SPOOSH

CAZENOVE & WILLIAM

24

AND THA' ONE...AND THA' ONE...

DO YOU KNOW WHAT THA' ONE MEANS?

EH, WHAT?

WELL, THIS SIGN MEANS YOU'RE FORBIDDEN TO PARK HERE, IN THIS SPOT...

NOT BAD!

NOT EVEN A SKATEBOARD OR A STROLLER...

AND THIS BLUE ONE, THERE, SAYS YOU NEED TO WATCH OUT FOR PEDESTRIANS, PEOPLE CROSSING ON THE WHITE LINES, YOU SEE?!

WELL, YES, I DO SEE.

YOU'RE TWO FOR TWO, I'D SAY.

AWESOME!

HANG ON. THIS SIGN HERE IS USED WHEN THERE'S A SPEEDING BUMP.

BUMP! BUMP! BUMP!

WRONG WAY...

YIELD...

WATCH OUT FOR TRAFFIC CIRCLES.

NO LEFT TURN...

ACTUALLY, READING SIGNS IS EASY-PEASY AND I NEVER EVER MAKE A MISTAKE!

OH, YEAH? REALLY NEVER EVER?

THEN YOU CAN TELL ME WHAT THIS SIGN THAT I HUNG ON THE DOOR TO MY ROOM MEANS!

HAH! VERY FUNNY!

CAZENOVE & WILLIAM

MAUREEN, I NEED YOUR OPINION...

WHICH DRESS SHOULD I WEAR TO THE PROM? I CAN'T DECIDE.

I LIKE THE RED ONE A LOT.

LOL! DO YOU WANT TO LOOK LIKE A BOTTLE OF KETCHUP?

÷BLERG!÷... SO, DID YOU LOSE THE REST OF THE DRESS SOMEWHERE?

HEE HEE HEE! DO THEY MAKE THE SAME MODEL FOR GIRLS?

YYYEEEAAAHH! SUPER CLASSY! SHREK'S DRESS! PICK THAT ONE! PICK THAT ONE!

—UGH!

WITH THAT ONE, YOU'LL BE THE BELLE OF HIGH SCHOOL... THE LUNCH BELL. BWAH-HA-HA!

HEY, MAUREEN, SHOULD I WEAR THE WHITE OR THE RED ONES, IN YOUR OPINION?

NOOO... YOU'RE GOING TO WEAR RUNNING SHOES TO GO TO THE PROM?

OF COURSE NOT. THIS IS TO CHASE YOU AND BEAT YOU UP!

IN MY OPINION, THAT'S A VERY BAD IDEA!

CAZENOVE & WILLIAM

YOU'RE AMAZING. I WISH IT WERE ALREADY HERE, SAMMIE...

...OUR FIRST PROM.

YES, I PUT ON MY DRESS... I WAS DYING TO WEAR IT. NOT TO BRAG, BUT I THINK I'M SOOO BEAUTIFUL IN IT.

I JUST HAVE TO ATTACH AN ORCHID FROM THE INSIDE, Y'KNOW?!

LA LA LA LA

THAT'S A REAL GROWNUP SECRET, LULU.

AN ORKIDLY ON YOUR DRESS, WOW! THAT HAS TO BE SO PRETTY.

BUT...DO YOU KNOW WHERE WE CAN FIND ONE?

YUP! MY MOM BOUGHT ONE AT THE MARKET THIS MORNING.

SO...CAN YOU GET IT TO WORK?

⸮PHEW.⸮ NOT YET.

HEY, WENDY, SERIOUSLY. HOW DO YOU GET YOUR ORKIDLY TO STAY ON?

THE POT JUST KEEPS SLIDING... EVEN WITH ADHESIVE PUTTY.

MWAH-HA-HA-HA!

CAZENOVE & WILLIAM

I NEVER GET BORED ON RAINY DAYS...

WENDY INVENTS SUCH AWESOME GAMES EVERY TIME...

THIS ONE'S CALLED *"CATCH WALLY, THE GIANT CROC."*

WOW! DOES HE HAVE REAL SHARK TEETH AND EVERYTHING?

LOL! I STILL HAVE TO CUT OUT THREE OF THEM.

WHO'RE THESE LI'L GUYS?

THE SCIENTISTS WHO ARE SUPPOSED TO BRING WALLY AND HIS FAMILY BACK...THERE ARE TWO HUNTERS TOO.

THIS IS SO GREAT!

GIVE ME ANOTHER FIVE MINUTES TO GLUE THE LITTLE GUYS ONTO THE PAPER AND CROC HUNT CAN BEGIN.

CAN YOUR GAME BE PLAYED BY ONE PERSON?

WHAT DO YOU MEAN BY ONE PERSON?

DO YOU THINK I SPENT HALF THE AFTERNOON MAKING THIS GAME TO NOT PLAY IT?

WELL, I WAS ASKING ABOUT THAT FOR YOU.

AS FOR ME, MY TV SHOW IS ABOUT TO BEGIN.

CLICK

HAPPY HUNTING!

CAZENOVE & WILLIAM

CAZENOVE ᴇᴛ WiLLiAM

HI, MAUR--

?!

HUFF PUFF

HUFF PUFF

HUFF PUFF

WELL, OKAY...

THAT LITTLE GIRL IS VERY ATHLETIC.

HI, WENDY! HEY, IS YOUR SISTER TRAINING FOR A MARATHON?

NO, SHE'S BEEN POKING AROUND IN MY THINGS AGAIN! THE PEST.

SHE'S OBVIOUSLY BEEN IN MY FACEBOOK ACCOUNT AND PASSED HERSELF OFF AS ME.

CAN YOU IMAGINE THAT?

BUT SHE KNOWS SHE'S GONE TOO FAR AND WHEN I CATCH HER, I'M GOING TO PULVERIZE HER...

WELL, OKAY, YOU KNOW HOW IT IS. I'M STRONGER AND FASTER THAN SHE IS!

AND THEN?

WAP

I ADMIT IT ISN'T VERY FAIR. AS A RESULT, I GIVE HER SEVERAL LAPS HEAD START.

PFFFF!

WENDY, WOULD YOU GIVE ME ANOTHER TWO LAPS, PLEASE?

CAZENOVE & WILLIAM

SNIFF!
BOO-HOO-
HOO!
SNIFF! SNIFF!

?

3:07

BOO-HOO!
SNIFF!
HOO-HOO!
SNIFF!
SNIFF!

WHA?
WHO?

SHHHH.
MAUREEN...IT'S
OKAY, MAUREEN,
IT'S NOTHING.

CALM
DOWN.

SNUFFLE. I HAD
SUCH AN AWFUL
NIGHTMARE.

HORRIFUL,
TOO.

I DREAMED
I MADE A BIIIG
MISTAKE...

WELL,
TELL ME
ABOUT IT.
THAT'LL BE
GOOD FOR
YOU.

AND THEN, YOU
TORTICRUSHED ME AND
REALLY, REALLY HURT
ME. YOU SCREAMED
AND SHOOK ME
LIKE A LEAF.

OH,
MAUREEN...

NEVER IN MY LIFE
WOULD I DO SUCH
HORRIBLE THINGS
TO YOU...

THAT'S
BARBARIC!

REALLY? EVEN
IF YOU FIND OUT
I ACCIDENTALLY
DROPPED YOUR
PHONE IN THE
TOILET?

HMMPH!

GRRRR!

THE PEST
IS GOOD...
REALLY
GOOD!

CAZENOVE & WILLIAM

WHO'S THAT TOTALLY UGLY LADY UP THERE, WENDY?

LOL! THAT'S NOT A LADY, MAUREEN. THAT'S *LOUIS XIV*, THE SUN KING. VERSAILLES. ALL THAT.

HE'S UGLY AS A GUY TOO.

AND OVER THERE YOU'VE GOT *JOAN OF ARC*, THE MAID OF ORLEANS, WHO BOOTED THE ENGLISH OUT OF FRANCE...BOOTED MEANS CHASED.

SHE DOESN'T LOOK THAT STRONG.

DO YOU THINK SHE PLAYED CATCH?

AND DO YOU KNOW WHO THIS IS?

OF COURSE. IT'S *NAPOLEON*.

AH, YES, HE CUT A FINE FIGURE. HE LEFT A BIG IMPRINT ON THE HISTORY OF FRANCE, Y'KNOW.

HE IS TOO COOL!

HEE HEE! I'M TALENTED AT EXPLAINING THINGS TO KIDS... MAYBE I SHOULD BECOME A TEACHER.

BUT, WENDY...

...WHO IS THE GUY SITTING ON TOP OF NAPOLEON?

OKAY, I GOT IT. I NEED TO FIND ANOTHER PROFESSION.

CAZENOVE & WILLIAM

SO, SUNDAY AT THE MUSEUM?

AWESOME!

LET *ME* TELL THEM! LET *ME* TELL THEM!

WE HAD HYSTERICAL FUN!

HUH?

WHAT?

SHE MEANS WE WENT TO THE HISTORICAL MUSEUM!

THAT'S 'ZACTLY WHAT I SAID. COPY CAT!

AND THEN WE SAW LOTS OF STATUES MADE OF FRONDS...

SHE MEANS: STATUES MADE OF BRONZE.

AFTERWARDS, MOM AND DAD LET US GO TO THE MULTI-SOCKET TO SEE AN SPYIFYING MOVIE.

MULTIPLEX... ...SPY MOVIE

OKAY, WELL, SO YOU HAD A BLAST, RIGHT?

DEFINITELY. I'M HAVING A BLAST WHEN YOU TELL US ABOUT IT, TOO!

WAIT! THERE'S MORE. I ALSO SAW MASON AND WENDY DO LOTS OF KISSY KISSY DURING THE MOVIE.

SMOOCH SMOOCH!

HEH HEH!

AH HA. OKAY, WENDY, WILL YOU TRANSLATE AGAIN?

OH, YES. WE'D LIKE TO KNOW MORE.

UMMM... I HAVE NO IDEA WHAT SHE MEANS.

≥TSSK≤... LIAR!

CAZENOVE & WILLIAM

COME ON, WENDY...

NO, NO, AND NO! PLUS EMMA AND SAMMIE ARE COMING HERE SO THAT WE CAN DO OUR REPORT.

IF YOU NEED TO GO TO THE LIBRARY, WELL, TAKE THE BUS ALL BY YOURSELF.

THE BUS ALL BY MYSELF?!

YOU'LL SEE. IT'S SUPER EASY.

I'LL EVEN GO WITH YOU TO THE STOP.

YOU'RE BIG NOW!

THE BUS ALL BY MYSELF...

GO ON, GET IN!

MAIN STREET

7777WM 12

YOU'VE GOT NOTHING TO LOSE.

YOU'RE SURE?

SEE YOU IN 45 MINUTES AT THE MOST.

IT'S TRUE THAT SHE'S GROWN QUICKLY.

WENDY, WENDY, WAIT... THE DRIVER DOESN'T WANT ME TO TAKE THE BUS ALL BY MYSELF.

SAY WHAT?

HE SAYS HE'S THE DRIVER. AND THAT THAT'S FINAL!

SUCH A MEANIE! ⸮HMPF!⸮

CAZENOVE & WILLIAM

TAP TAP TAP

POWER

SHAKA BOOOM BOOM BOOOM

SHAKA BOOOM

CLICK

RRRR

KRR

RR

RRR KRR

R RRRK

WOOOO SHAKA BOOM BOOM BOOOM BOOM

KRRR RRR

BOOM RORR RRK RD RRRIP

KRRR WOOO OORR

OOO KRR WOOO

SCRTCH

TAGADA

I WANT ONE!

I WANT ONE!

I WANT ONE!

=ARF!=

=ARF!=

SO, IT'S NOT THE SOUND THAT ATTRACTS HER... MAYBE THE SMELL?!

CAZENOVE & WILLIAM

CAZENOVE & WILLIAM

MY SISTER MAUREEN IS REALLY GENEROUS...

MAUREEEEN...

MAUREEEEN...

CAN YOU LEND ME YOUR FELT BRUSHES? THE SET WITH ALL THE COLORS IN IT, YOU KNOW?

NO PROBLEMO, LULU.

PLUS, I WANTED TO GO SKATEBOARDING THIS AFTERNOON BUT CAN'T FIND...COULD YOU...?

NO WORRIES. I'LL GO GET IT FOR YOU.

CAN I BORROW YOUR HEADPHONES TO LISTEN TO SOME TUNES? THAT'D BE FABULOUS...

HERE, WATER THE FLOWERS...

I'LL BRING EVERYTHING HERE.

SHE'S SO COOL. COURSE, SHE'S MY BFF.

HERE YOU GOOOO... LOOK, EVERYTHING YOU ASKED ME FOR IS IN THIS BOX!

AWESOOOME! HEY, I FORGOT. COULD YOU ALSO LEND ME YOUR LITTLE PURPLE ROUND-TIPPED SCISSORS?

AHH, NO, NO, NO. THOSE SCISSORS ARE MINE, NOT MY SISTER'S.

ACTUALLY, MAUREEN IS MOSTLY GENEROUS WITH MY THINGS.

CAZENOVE & WILLIAM

DADDYYYY... THERE'S NO MORE WATER!

IT'S A DISASTER. LOOK...IT'S NOT WORKING ANYMORE.

OH, WENDY, THAT'S SO LIKE YOU...

...THE MOMENT YOU HAVE A PROBLEM, YOU CALL FOR HELP INSTEAD OF THINKING.

YES, WELL, ≥PFF≤, HEY...

WHEREAS IF YOU HAD TAXED YOUR GRAY MATTER A BIT, YOU COULD HAVE LOOKED FARTHER BACK ALONG THE HOSE...

AND YOU WOULD HAVE SEEN THAT IT WAS JUST CRIMPED.

YOU UNCRIMP IT AND THE WATER COMES OUT AGAIN. MAGIC, EH?!

AH, HUH. THANKS FOR THE ADVICE, DADDY!

SO, MAUREEN... WE HAVEN'T GOT ALL DAY!

WHAT'S THE ANSWER?

I THINK I'VE GOT A HOSE TO UNCRIMP IN MY HEAD...IF I DON'T GO BACK A BIT TOWARDS THE BEND, THE SOLUTION WON'T FLOW.

$5 + 5 =$
$8 + 1 =$
$2 + 3 =$
$2 + 3 + 1 =$
$3 + 1 + 1 =$

SKRIIITCH

CAZENOVE & WILLIAM

PSHSHHHH...

PSHHHHHHH...

PSHHHHHH...

SHHHHH

PSHHHHHH...

YES! I'VE GOT IT!

PSHHHH...

DON'T WORRY, WENDY...

IF YOUR SPRAY DOESN'T WORK...

I'LL GET THAT AWFUL MOSQUITO WITH MY FLYSWATTER!

CAZENOVE & WILLIAM

PHOOEY... I'VE GOT A CRAZY DAY AHEAD OF ME...

HOW ABOUT YOU, MAUREEN?

?!

THE BUS IS HERE, MAUR--

?!

ARE YOU ALMOST DONE WITH YOUR HOMEWORK SO WE CAN PLAY A LITTLE?

THERE'S A GOOD MOVIE ON TONIGHT, I THINK. HEY, MAUREEN?

I SENSE THAT YOU'RE GOING TO CONK OUT PRETTY SOON.

BRUSH BRUSH BRUSH

YOU WERE ZONKED OUT ALL DAY LONG.

HEY, HUH? NO, NO, NOT AT ALL. IF ANYTHING, I TRIED TO FALL ASLEEP BUT COULDN'T.

IT BUGS ME!

SO, HOW COME?

I HAD A TOTALLY AWESOME DREAM LAST NIGHT AND I REALLY WANTED TO KNOW WHAT HAPPENS NEXT.

BRUSH BRUSH BRUSH

CAZENOVE & WILLIAM

ANOTHER ONE, DADDY. YOUR SAUCY-GUESSES ARE SO GOOD. YUM!

"SAUSAGES" NOT "SAUCY-GUESSES." ⊰ARRGH.⊱ YOU'RE SO LAME!

AND I'LL HAVE THE BIGGEST *CHAR-LIZARD.*

CHORIZO!

YOU'RE EXHAUSTING, WHEN YOU SAY THINGS ANY WHICH WAY, Y'KNOW?!

YOU'RE THE ONE WHO HAS HER HEARS STOPPED UP, INSTEAD.

YOU'RE JEALOUS 'CUZ I'M SO TALENTED AT BARBATUNE.

BARBECUE, NOT BARBATUNE!

WENDY, WHAT WOULD YOU LIKE?

GREAT! I'M STARVING.

SO, I'D LIKE A...

...A...

I WANT...

⊰ARGGH!⊱...NICE JOB! I CAN'T REMEMBER THE NAME NOW.

WOULD YOU LIKE A LITTLE OF MY SAUCY-GUESSES?!

CAZENOVE & WILLIAM

BRINGIE BRINGIEE
BRING
BRINGIE
BRINGIEE
BRING
BRING
VRRRRRRRRR

QUICK! QUICK! QUICK!

STOMP STOMP STOMP

⸗MMMPH!⸗... WHAT'S ALL THAT RACKET? THERE'S NO WAY TO SLEEP PEACEFULLY WITH ALL THIS RUCKUS.

I HAVE TO GET READY FOR THE DANCE TONIGHT...

...SO I'D REALLY LIKE TO GET IN THE BATHROOM BEFORE YOU.

BUT TO DO THAT, I HAVE TO GET UP EARLY, RIGHT?!

I SWEAR, YOU COMPLAIN TO DEATH ABOUT EVERYTHING.

DO NOT!

YESTERDAY EVENING, I GOT EVERYTHING I NEEDED TO GET READY AND PUT IT IN MY ROOM.

SHAMPOO, SOAP, COMB, AND EVEN MY TOOTHBRUSH.

HEY, PEST, DID YOU THINK ABOUT GETTING IN THE TUB TOO?

LET ME IIIIIIN... I HAVE TO GET READY FOR THE DAAAAANCE...

BAM BA BADAM

BADAM BOM

BAM BADAM

OCCUPIED.

E & WILLIAM

44

HEY, HANDSOME, THEY'RE PLAYING A SLOW DANCE NOW...

EH? UH, WELL, SLOW DANCES, UH, WELL, I DON'T KNOW...

IT'S *ME!*

HE WANTS TO DANCE WITH ME!

HEY, MASON?! AND AFTER THIS DANCE, WE'LL DO ANOTHER TO ROUND THINGS UP, AND ANOTHER ONE TO SAY GOODBYE AND THEN...

UMMMM... BUUUT...I... DON'T...

GET YOUR DIRTY PAWS OFF MY DANCE PARTNER. YOU'RE GOING TO GET HIM ALL DIRTY.

≥PHEWWW!≤

HEEEEY, DON'T TOUCH ME!

YOU'RE JUST JEALOUS!

MASON PREFERS TO BE WITH A GOOD DANCER ...

...NOT WITH A CINDER BLOCK WHO'S AS STIFF AS A STICK.

DO YOU KNOW WHAT THAT CINDER BLOCK IS GOING TO DO WITH HER STICK?

MASON IS DANCING THE WHOLE NIGHT WITH ME. PERIOD!

YOU'RE JUST A LEECH!

HURRY, HURRY. LET'S GET TO THE DANCE FLOOR TO GET AWAY FROM HER...

PERHAPS WE CAN EVEN DANCE TO A SONG OR TWO...?!

AH, OKAY, FOR SURE.

...STILL, HAVING A LITTLE SISTER REALLY COMES IN HANDY SOMETIMES.

CAZENOVE & WILLIAM

TSSSK...SHE'S GOING TO WIND UP SPOILING MY EVENING, I SWEAR...

Boo-Hooo-Hooo.. Boo-Hooo Hoo Hoo SNIFF

ROOM ROOM ROOM

OKAY *OKAY*, OKAY! STOP THE WATERWORKS... I'LL GO GET YOU ONE. IT'S OKAY. ⇒ARRRGH!⇐...

SPRING PROM

GRUMBLE

STRAWBERRY ICE CREAM, PLEASE.

ONE SCOOP OR TWO, SWEETHEART?

COZY

BUT, WENDY, WHY DID YOU BUY MAUREEN ICE CREAM...?

...EVEN THOUGH SHE WANTED YOU TO BRING HER PERFUME?

SAMMIE, YOU KNOW MY SISTER...

AND YOU KNOW ALL TOO WELL THAT SHE NEVER DOES ANYTHING LIKE ANYONE ELSE.

GROSS!

SPLOTCH

SPLITCH

YOU CAN TAKE A LITTLE, LULU, IF YOU WANT TO SMELL GOOD, TOO.

CAZENOVE & WILLIAM

46

I'VE REALLY BEEN LOOKING FORWARD TO THIS PROM...

...EVER SINCE I DREAMED ABOUT IT...

WOW! THAT WAS THE BEST PARTY OF MY WHOLE LIFE!

CAZENOVE & WILLIAM

MAUREEN, YOU'LL NEVER GUESS WHAT I FOUND AT THE BOTTOM OF MY BOX.

UMMM, YOUR FIRST RETAINER?!

LOL. OF COURSE NOT. THE DRESS I WORE TO THAT FANTASTIC PROM. DO YOU REMEMBER IT?

TOTALLY! AND MASON DEVOURING YOU WITH HIS EYES.

FIRST PROM, FIRST DRESS, FIRST AND LAST TIME I WANTED TO DANCE A WALTZ, TOO.

HA HA! THE FUNKY CHICKEN, FOR ME.

MMMMMM... AND IT STILL SMELLS OF OUR SCENTS, A SWEET MIXTURE OF FRUITY AND WILD AROMAS.

LET ME SEE...

SNURF SNURF

MMMMM... WHAT A PARTY!

AND ME, TOO! I FOUND MY DRESS.

GREAT! AND DOES IT HAVE THE SAME SCENT?

NO, BUT IT'S FULL OF MEMORIES.

GET A LOAD OF THIS! IT STILL HAS PIECES OF PIZZA, AND STAINS FROM ICE CREAM, AND CHOCOLATE...

MMMMM... WHAT A PARTY!

BLURF

CAZENOVE & WILLIAM

WHEN I WAS AN ONLY CHILD, IT SEEMED LIKE...

WAH HOOO!

BONK

HA HA HA!

WLMP

WLMP

WLMP

WLMP

...I RAN EVERYWHERE AND JUMPED ALL OVER THE PLACE...

YEHAAAH!

I WAS A REAL LIVE WIRE. ALWAYS IN MOTION...TIRELESS...

WWAAAH!

?!

BUT AS SOON AS MAUREEN WAS BORN, I CALMED DOWN.

WWAAAAH!

AWWW...DON'T CRY LITTLE BABY...YOUR BIG SISTER'S HERE!

I BECAME BETTER BEHAVED, MORE RESPONSIBLE...

STOP RIGHT THERE...

CAREFUL! YOU'RE GOING TO GET YOUR FINGERS CAUGHT IN THE DOOR.

DOE?!

...AND MY SISTER BECAME THE REAL LIVE WIRE.

WEE! HEE-WEE!

WEE!

NO, SERIOUSLY, YOU NEED TO MAKE ANOTHER BABY TO CALM MAUREEN DOWN...

I'VE HAD IT!

CAZENOVE & WILLIAM

TADAAAA!

A PRESENT FOR MY SISTER!

OH, GEEZ! YOUR DRAWING'S SO BEAUTIFUL, WENDY. I LOOOOVE IT!

BUT MY BIRTHDAY WAS YESTERDAY ...

AND YOU ALREADY GAVE ME A REALLY PRETTY DRAWING.

SO, WHAT'S THE PROBLEM?

YOU KNOW THAT I LIKE TO MAKE THINGS TO SURPRISE MY SISTER, WHO I LOVE.

HEE-HEE

BESIDES, I JUST DECREED THAT *EVERY DAY* IS MY BELOVED LI'L MAUREEN'S BIRTHDAY.

NO, FOR REALS?!

EVERY DAY IN *EVERY MONTH* OF THE YEAR WILL BE MY BIRTHDAY WITH KISSES AND PRESENTS?!

GAAAHH...

I HAVE THE BEST BIG SISTER IN THE WHOLE UNIVERSE!

EVERY DAY *EXCEPT* APRIL 18, OF COURSE, BECAUSE THAT'S *MY* BIRTHDAY.

YOU'RE SO SELFISH!

WHATEVS! ⇒PFF!⇐ ...

VERO, CAZENOVE & WILLI

50

HEY, WENDY, DO YOU WANT TO PLAY "ROBOSSANDRO BEAUTY SALON" WITH ME?

CAN'T YOU SEE I'M A BIT BUSY HERE? YOU CAN DO YOUR HAIR ALL BY YOURSELF.

OKAY, LET'S GET BACK TO OUR PHOTO ALBUM, MASON DEAR.

POOH!

LOL! GET A LOAD OF WHAT MAUREEN LOOKS LIKE WHEN SHE POUTS.

TOO CUTE, DON'T YOU THINK?

IT'S OKAY. YOU DON'T HAVE TO TALK TO ME ABOUT YOUR SISTER ALL THE TIME...

ARE YOU TALKING TO ME WITH THAT TONE OF VOICE, MASE?

Y'KNOW, IF WE KEEP SEEING EACH OTHER, YOU'LL PROBABLY RUN INTO MY SISTER A LOT...

...SO YOU MAY AS WELL GET USED TO IT RIGHT AWAY, MY MAN.

THAT WAS FIRST OF ALL...

SECOND OF ALL, I'LL SPEAK ABOUT *WHO* I WANT *WHEN* I WANT AND YOU'RE CERTAINLY NOT THE ONE WHO--

?!?!

TOO CUTE!

AWWWW... HE'S SO KEWT...

LOOK HOW PRETTY THIS KITTYCATKINS IS.

IT LOOKS LIKE YOU LOVE BEING PETTED?!

MEOW PURRR PURRR....

HEE-HEE. LOOK HOW HE'S RUBBING UP AGAINST ME...

MEOW

HE TOTALLY LIKES ME.

I'D SAY HE'S MARKING HIS TERRITORY, INSTEAD.

WHAT? HE'S WRITING ON ME?!

BY RUBBING UP AGAINST YOU, HE LEAVES HIS SCENT ON YOU AND WHEN HE SEES YOU AGAIN, THAT HELPS HIM RECOGNIZE YOU.

ACTUALLY, FOR THE CAT, THAT MEANS YOU'RE HIS.

LOL

?? ??

ZOOM

HEE-HEE. HEADS UP: I'VE RUBBED UP AGAINST ALL YOUR COMICS...

YOUR CLOTHES...

YOUR DVDS, YOUR CDS, YOUR DRESSER, YOUR BED...

EVERYTHING'S MINE NOW!

RUB RUB RUB RUB

CAZENOVE & WILLIAM

52

SO, ARE YOU UP FOR DOING THE "PORTNAWAK RUN"?

TOTALLY.

IT LOOKS REALLY COOL!

I'M IN TO THE MAX WITH ALL OF YOU, TOO!

YIKES, WE WEREN'T PLANNING ON THAT.

Y'KNOW, MAUREEN... THE "PORTNAWAK RUN" IS CHOCK FULL OF THINGS YOU DON'T LIKE AT ALL...

LIKE... ORIENTEERING, FOR EXAMPLE.

PLUS WE'LL BE HAULING AROUND HEAVY PACKS ON OUR BACK THE WHOLE DAY...

WE'RE GOING TO SWEAT MORE THAN IN THE MIDDLE OF SUMMER UNDER A QUILT.

SINCE WE'LL HAVE TO SLEEP WHERE WE ARE, ADIOS TO OUR FAVORITE TV SERIES!

PHOOEY!

AND WE'LL BE SO WIPED OUT THAT WE WON'T EVEN HAVE THE ENERGY TO READ A COMICBOOK BEFORE GOING TO SLEEP.

HEY, OKAY. YOUR COURSE IS TOTALLY ROTTEN... YOU CAN GO WITHOUT ME!

~YES!~

WE'RE RID OF THE LEECH!

NOT TO MENTION THAT IT'LL BE CRAMMED FULL OF INSECTS AND THAT WE'LL HAVE TO WADE THROUGH THE MUD.

WAY TO GO, SAMMIE!

YEAH! BRAVO!

HEH HEH

WHERE'S THE MUD?

WHERE IS IT?

CAZENOVE & WILLIAM

HEY THERE, SISTERS!

NOOO...

I CAN'T BELIEVE IT...

YOU'RE HERE ALREADY?!

CAMIILLE...

HEE HEE HEE, WHAT A WELCOME!

MY FAVORITE COUSIN WHO I LOVE SO MUCH MORE THAN ANYONE ELSE...YIPPIE!

I KNEW YOU WERE GOING TO BE VISITEDING.

THAT DESERVES A GREAT BIG SNUGGLE COMBINED WITH 1000 CUDDLES, RIGHT?!

BIG SNUGGLE
BIG SNUGGLE
BIG SNUGGLEE

OOF!

ARGH! MAUREEN...

STOOOP!

I GET IT. IT'S ALRIGHT. I'M HAPPY YOU'RE GLAD TO SEE ME, OKAY! NOW, GO PLAY SOMEWHERE ELSE.

AND ON TOP OF THAT, YOU SEND ME PACKING! WOOOW! YOU'RE REALLY LIKE A SISTER.

BWAHAHA

WHAT A GOOF!

CAZENOVE & WILLIAM

SO, ARE YOU READY, GIRLS?

YES, JUST A SEC, WENDY...

PHOOEY...DO YOU REALLY HAVE TO LUG AROUND THOSE GINORMIOUS BIG PACKS?

IT LOOKS SUPER HEAVY.

WELL, YOU SEE, IT'S THE MINIMUM GEAR FOR ALL PARTICIPANTS... SPARE SHOES, MAPS, COMPASS...

SOMETHING TO EAT AND DRINK, TO LIGHT A FIRE IF NECESSARY, THREADS, A MIRROR, BLANKET, A SMALL FOLDING SHOVEL, ETC., ETC.

BUT WE'RE NOT GOING TO COVER MILLIONS OF MILES TODAY...

ESPECIALLY SINCE YESTERDAY WE GOT REALLY WORN OUT...

THAT'S TRUE.

YOU'RE RIGHT, MAUREEN...

I DON'T NECESSARILY HAVE TO TAKE MY PACK FOR THIS LITTLE TREK.

YEE-HAW!

GIDDYAP! LET'S GO!

HOLD ON WHAT? BUT--

HUP! LET'S GO, HORSEY!

FORWARD!

GO! GO! GO!

I'VE TOTALLY BEEN HAD.

TAP TAP

CAZENOVE & WILLIAM

ATTENTION... THE NEXT RACE STARTS...

...IN FIVE MINUTES.

OH, HEY! YOUR SISTER'S GOT A REAL PROBLEM.

SHE'S SCREAMING AT EVERYONE FOR NO REASON AT ALL.

PAY NO ATTENTION TO HER, SAMMIE.

I ADVISED HER TO WARM UP BEFORE EACH RACE, SO SHE'S WARMING UP.

UMM...YEAH. WELL, AS A RESULT, SHE'S GOTTEN EVERYONE REALLY STEAMED.

CAZENOVE & WILLIAM

READY...

GO ON, WENDY, YOU'RE GOING TO **CRUSH** THEM!

ROC T CANON The Nawak'Run

...GET SET...

OFF YOU GO! LUCKY KISS.

SMACK

GO!

GO, WENDY! GO, WENDY!

BOING BOING

YES!

WENDY'S THE WINNER!

MAUREEN, ARE YOU COMING?

OUR RACE IS GOING TO START...

YES... JUST A SEC...

WAK RUN

AAHH, THERE YOU ARE, MASEY...

I'LL CRUSH EVERYONE, THANKS TO YOUR **LUCKY KISS,** ISN'T THAT RIGHT?!

I'M READY!

MMUMM...

HEY, BUT...

IT WAS TO HELP ME RUN!

HYDRATE

CAZENOVE & WILLIAM

I THINK I KNOW WHICH RACE YOUR SISTER'S GOING TO DO, WENDY...

GL...GLUG GLUG

HMM?

IT HAS TO BE *HIGH ROPES*. IT'S A SICK COURSE.

⋛BZZT!⋚ ...ALL WRONG!

COME ON, TRY AGAIN...

UMMM, MAYBE AN ORIENTEERING COURSE?!

WITH ALL THESE HUGE BOULDERS, IT'S LOGICAL.

⋛BZZT!⋚... STILL NOT THAT.

THE HEDGE LABYRINTH, THEN?

THERE'RE LOTS OF CRITTERS AND SHE LIKES *THOSE*.

HA HA. YOU'RE THINKING TOO HARD, GIRLS...

SHE JUST WANTS TO JOIN THE COURSE THERE, PLAIN AND SIMPLE...

OKAY, WHY?

THERE'S *MUD* THERE!

HA HA

OOH, HEYYYY!

CAZENOVE & WILLIAM

AND BECAUSE OF *YOU*, OUR TEAM CAME IN LAST!

EXCUSE ME?

MY FAULT AGAIN?! YOU *ALWAYS* BLAME ME!

OBVIOUSLY! YOU'RE A WALKING *DISASTER!*

SINCE YOU FEEL THAT WAY, I'M NO LONGER YOUR SISTER!

GREAT! I'D LOVE TO BE AN ONLY CHILD AGAIN.

STOP!

AREN'T YOU SICK OF YELLING ALL THE TIME?

A DAY DOESN'T GO BY THAT I DON'T HAVE A RINGSIDE SEAT TO YOUR LAME CIRCUS!

MMPPFF

YOU DON'T EVEN REALIZE HOW LUCKY YOU ARE.

THAT'S WHAT BUGS ME!

I DO *NOT* HAVE A SISTER...

AND I SERIOUSLY MISS OUT ON HAVING ONE.

YOU SHOULD THINK ABOUT THAT FOR A COUPLE OF MINUTES.

I'LL TAKE SAMMIE FOR A SISTER!

LET GO OF HER!

MOVE! SHE'S MINE!

LEEEET GO LEEEE...

GNNNN

CAZENOVE & WILLIAM

OKAY, THEN, WENDY, WHERE'RE WE GOING TO PITCH OUR TENT?

YEAH, WE'VE BEEN GOING AROUND HERE FOR AGES...

WE'RE NOT GOING TO JUST SETTLE IN ANYWHERE. WE JUST HAVE TO MOVE QUICKLY, YOU KNOW...

SO WHY NOT HERE, THEN?

CERTAINLY NOT HERE... IT'S ALREADY INHABITED BY BILLIONS OF FILTHY CREATURES.

NOPE! TOO CLOSE TO THE RIVER...

IF IT OVERFLOWS, WE'VE HAD IT.

MUCH TOO MUCH WIND AROUND HERE.

YOU CAN SAY THAT AGAIN!

NOT HERE EITHER... IF THE ROCKS TUMBLE DOWN, WE'LL WAKE UP AS FLAT AS PANCAKES.

HERE, THIS IS PERFECT!

THE BEST OF THE BEST!

WE REALLY HAD TO LOOK AROUND A BIT... RIGHT, GIRLS?

THIS IS THE PERFECT SPOT!

CAZENOVE & WILLIAM

≈PFFF...≈

??

?

≈AHEM!≈ ≈COUGH!≈
≈COUGH!≈ HEY...
≈PSST!≈ BRAT...

≈SHHHH!≈

ARE YOU GOING TO DECIDE ALREADY? WINTER'LL BE HERE SOON IF YOU KEEP THIS UP.

HERE. PITCH TENT. YOU CAN.

WELL, HEY, IT'S ABOUT TIME.

WENDY, WHAT'S YOUR SISTER LISTENING FOR? WHETHER ANY COWBOYS ARE COMING?

IF ONLY...

ACTUALLY, SHE JUST WANTS TO REASSURE HERSELF THAT WE'RE NOT GOING TO HURT HER DARLING LITTLE INSECTS WHEN WE SET THE TENT STAKES.

NO, NO NO, CAMILLE... NOT THERE. THERE'S A WHOLE FAMILY OF MAGGOTS LIVING THERE!

?!

CAZENOVE & WILLIAM

NO, REALLY, I'M JUST EXPLAINING TO YOU. THIS HAPPENED LAST WEEKEND A STONE'S THROW FROM THE VIADUCT...

CRACK

CRACK

YAHAAH

CRACK

MAUREEN WAS PLAYING KARATE KID OF THE SAVANNA AND SMASHED EVERYTHING AROUND HER...

MAUREEN... STOP BREAKING ALL THE BRANCHES LIKE THAT.

OH...COME ON! A TREE IS A LIVING BEING AND YOU *JUST* MADE IT SUFFER.

THAT JOKE'S NOT FUNNY.

I'M NOT JOKING... IT'S AWARE, YOU KNOW.

I FEEL YOUR SUFFERING.

PHOOEY!... YOU'RE SAYING THAT TO ACT LIKE A GROWN-UP.

DO YOU SEE THIS LIQUID? IT'S *SAP* FROM THE TREE. IT'S LIKE OUR BLOOD.

BUUU--BUT. I DIDN'T KNOW THAT. AND CAN WE HEAL IT?

LUCKILY I ALWAYS HAVE A FIRST AID KIT IN MY PACK.

I'M SO SORRY, MR. TREE. I WAS TOO YOUNG TO KNOW I GAVE YOU A BOOBOO.

100% TROUBLE

I KNOW. I KNOW. I NEED TO STOP WANTING TO TEACH MAUREEN THINGS...

DON'T WORRY ABOUT ANYTHING, MY LI'L *TREESIES*. I'LL *TAKE CARE* OF ALL OF YOU MYSELF.

SO, LEAVE WITHOUT US... OTHERWISE, I HAVE A FEELING THIS TREK IS GOING TO LAST FOR HOURS.

CAZENOVE & WILLIAM

AND THAT'S WHEN THE ZOMBIE SUDDENLY LOOMED OUT OF THE FOREST. *BWAHHAAAAHA!...* IT CAUGHT THE CAMPERS...

...AND DRAGGED THEM TO THE BOTTOM OF THE DECAYING LAKE...⹂BLUB!⹂ ⹂BLUB!⹂...

⹂PHEW!⹂... FREAKY!

THAT'S EVEN SCARIER THAN THE STORY OF "THE WOMAN IN WHITE" THAT *ALANIS* TOLD.

YOU'RE CLEARLY THE BEST AT SCARING US, WENDY.

MY TURN, MY TURN, MY TURN, MY TURN. YOU'LL SEE WHO SCARES EVERYONE THE MOST.

OOOO! I'M SO *SCARED*...I'LL TRY NOT TO LAUGH.

IT'S NOT GOING TO BE EASY TO DO BETTER THAN THESE TWO CLASSIC HORROR STORIES.

I THINK YOU COULD EVEN SKIP YOUR TURN.

MY STORY WON'T TAKE LONG...

SO, TO BEGIN. WE'RE REALLY SLEEPING TOGETHER IN THE SAME TENT TONIGHT, RIGHT?

WELL, YEAH, BUT YOUR STORY'S GOT A ROTTEN BEGINNING, ALREADY.

WAIT, WENDY...HERE, IT'S BEEN ABOUT TWO WEEKS SINCE I'VE CHANGED MY SOCKS...

AAAAAH...ARGH!

WHO'S THE BEST AT SCARING EVERYONE NOW?

NOOO!

HELP!

LET ME OUT! LET ME OUT!

CAZENOVE & WILLIAM

CAZENOVE & WILLIAM

YEEHAAAAH...

COLD!

BRR
BRR   BRR

⊰BRR BRR!⊱...WEN-
WEN-WEN-WENDY...⊰BRR!⊱...
WOU-WOULD YOU
HAVE SOMETHING
TO-TO-TO WARM
ME UP?

AH HA, YOU'RE VERY
HAPPY TO HAVE YOUR
BIG SISTER...WHO THINKS
OF EVERYTHING...
WITH *YOU*, ISN'T
THAT SO?

FOR-FOR-
FOR SURE!

HERE, IT'LL BE A
LOT BETTER WITH
SOME NICE HOT
CHOCOLATE.

THA-
THA-THA-
THANKS!

IT'S OKAY
NOW. YOU CAN
COME SWIM...

IT'LL BE
A GOOD
TEMPERATURE
SOON.

CAZENOVE & WILLIAM

YAWN!

BOO!

EEEEEEEEK!

ARGHHH! STOP WAVING THAT HORROR UNDER MY NOSE. YOU KNOW HOW MUCH I HATE THAT.

HA HA!

I GOT YOU GOOD! GODZILLA, ATTACK!

NOW I ITCH ALL OVER. WAY TO GO.

GET THAT OUT OF MY SIGHT!

I'VE GOT HUGE GOOSEBUMPS, TOO! LOOK.

AH-HA! HEE-HEE! TEE-HEE!

STOP! I'M TELLING YOU. I'M NOT JOKING AROUND ANYMORE. GET RID OF THAT VILE THINGIE.

WHOA, HEY. IT'S OKAY IF WE CAN'T JOKE AROUND ANYMORE.

I'M NOT TALKING TO *YOU*, BUT RATHER TO THE SCARAB.

?!!

BUT UMMM... I'M NOT A *VIIIILE* THINGIE...

WAAAAHHHH!

WHOA, HEY, IT'S OKAY IF WE CAN'T JOKE AROUND ANYMORE.

CAZENOVE & WILLIAM

THIS HIKE OF YOURS IS HARD, WENDY.

I KNOW. I DID IT ON PURPOSE. I SCOUTED IT OUT **3 DAYS AGO.**

AH. THAT'S SOMETHING ELSE, THEN ...

YOU'LL UNDERSTAND, SAMMIE...WE'RE GOING TO GET TO A TREE THAT'S LYING ON THE GROUND.

SO?

SO, I'LL PRETEND TO SLIP AND ZIP! MASON WILL CATCH ME IN HIS ARMS...BINGO! INSTANT KISS, YOU KNOW.

HEE-HEE

SMART! HEY, THERE'S YOUR TREE RIGHT OVER THERE.

WHOA...BUT THIS OBSTACLE... ⇒PHEW!⇐...HUP, ONE, TWO...

THIS ONE'S REALLY WIDE.

YIKES! I'M SLIPPING. I'M GOING TO--I'M GOING TO--I'M GOING TO TUMB--

--BLE!

OW!

LET ME HELP YOU!

YES, SAFETY FIRST! DON'T LET ME FALL...LIKE WENDY!

CAZENOVE & WILLIAM

THE ANTS GO MARCHING THREE BY THREE...HURRAH HURRAH...THE ANTS GO MARCHING 'CROSS MY FEET, HURRAH, HURRAH...

OOPS! WAIT, WENDY, I FORGOT MY WATER BOTTLE.

FIVE MINUTES LATER...

HERE IT IS! HERE IT IS! AND I BROUGHT BACK YOUR iPOD....

I REALLY LOVE WALKING TO MUSIC...

OH, RATS. I NEED MY SKETCHBOOK, TOO...

YOU NEVER KNOW WHEN THERE'LL BE CUTE SQUIRRELS.

GRUMFF

HERE! AND I BROUGHT YOUR PENCILS, IN CASE YOU WANT TO COLOR WITH ME.

YIKES! I SHOULD'VE THOUGHT TO BRING SOME COOKIES. DON'T MOVE!

OTHERWISE, I'LL BE TOO HUNGRY.

OOOOF!

OKAY, TAKE YOUR TIME THEN!

WE'VE GOT ALL DAY, AFTER ALL!

YES, YES, OKAY, OKAY... ÷WHEW!÷

BUT...COULD WE TAKE A BREAK HERE?

I'M WIPED OUT.

HUFF

PUFF

CAZENOVE & WILLIAM

CONKED OUT... KAPUT... WORN OUT.

EXHAUSTED... RUN DOWN... RUBBERY...

꓿HUFF!꓿ THESE OBSTACLE COURSES KILL ME.

CLEARLY! IT'S NOT FOR BIG FAT SOFTIES.

ANYWAY, WITHOUT REALIZING IT, WE CLIMBED MILES OF TREE TRUNKS.

AND WE RAN OVER TENS OF ZILLIONS OF ROCKS, DIDN'T WE?!

PERSONALLY, MY ONLY GOAL RIGHT NOW...

IS THE...

SO...

...FA...

...AH!

꓿ARGH!꓿... MY FEET!

WE CAN FINALLY GET BACK TO OUR *NORMAL* ACTIVITIES.

AH, YES, TOTALLY!

YEEAAH! PUT THE PEDAL TO THE METALS!

WHAT'LL WE PLAY? WHAT'LL WE PLAY?

CAN I JUMP ON YOUR BED? CAN WE PLAY CATCH?

NO, NO, *NOOOOO!* I DIDN'T SAY ANYTHING! I DIDN'T SAY ANYTHING!

CAZENOVE & WILLIAM

MY COUSIN CAMILLE IS LIKE A SISTER TO ME...

FARTHER, MUCH MUCH FAAAARTHER...

WE'RE REALLY ON THE SAME WAVELENGTH.

WE'RE JUST SO SO A MA ZING :)...

LET'S C A MOVIE 2 MORROW?! ♥♥

WE WIND UP HAVING CRAZY FUN...

I'M YOUR FATHER... YOUNG SKYWALKER.

HA! HA! HA! HA! HA!

I CAN'T DESCRIBE IT BETTER: SHE'S LIKE A SISTER.

MWAHAHA! LOOK AT THOSE MUGS!

LOL

HA! HA! HA!

⋛CHZG CHOMP MUNCH MORF CHR CHOR ZOHRZ?⋛

⋛OOH ARARARA CH VCH MOECH CM MOO VCMARCHX!⋛

AR! AR! AR!

⋛VCHO SHEE CRAPOTCH-CHIPCHS!⋛

CHIVE CHIVE MORPHON!

CORRECTION...

CHOMPF CHIMARK! HEER HEER!

⋛MEEOCHEEV MIAM CHOMPCH GOBBLOCH HEER HEER HEER!⋛

??

NOBODY'S LIKE MY SISTER!

CAZENOVE & WILLIAM

OKAY, WENDY, ARE YOU GOING TO PLAY OR NOT?

JUST A SEC, CAMILLE.

HEY, BRAT...

UNLESS I'M WRONG, YOU LOOK LIKE SOMEONE WHO'S ABOUT TO PULL A LAME PRANK?!

HEE-HEE! YES! YES! HEE-HEE!

I'M GOING TO SCARE THE LIVING DAYLIGHT OUT OF ALANIS WITH THIS PLASTIC SPIDER.

HAIRY CREEPY CRAWLIES GIVE HER HORROR-HIVES.

HA! HA! HA!

UMM, I WOULDN'T IF I WERE YOU.

OH, BOO-HOO... AREN'T I ALLOWED TO FOOL AROUND A BIT?

MAUREEN, NO...

EEEEE

EEEEEEEE

WE TRIED TO WARN HER THAT IT'S SUPER DANGEROUS TO MAKE ALANIS SCREAM...

DIDN'T WORK...

BUT EVERYONE IN THE FAMILY KNOWS THIS?!

THERE YOU GO...

NOW, LISTEN TO MUSIC THAT ISN'T SO LOUD, YOUNG LADY.

CAZENOVE & WILLIAM

WENDY, WOULD YOU--

NO TIME TO PLAY "DOCTOR HORRIBLE" WITH YOU. I'M LABELING MY PHOTOS FROM THE RACE YESTERDAY.

BUUUUT...I'M REALLY HURTING AND IT'S NO LAUGHING MATTER!

BLA BLA BLA BLA BLA BLA BLA BLA BLA BLA

YOU'LL HAVE TO CUT IT OFF! YOU DON'T NEED ME FOR THAT... HA-HA!

MY ARMS FEEL SO TIGHT THAT I CAN'T GRAB THE JAR OF NULTELA THAT'S HIDDEN IN THE PANTRY!

AND MY CALVES FEEL EVEN WORSE...

BLA BLA BLA BLA

AND IT FEELS LIKE I'VE GOT NEEDLES JABBING ME IN MY BACK...

I THINK I'VE CAUGHT A DISEASE YOU NEED TO MASSCULPT!

PHEW. MWAH-HA-HA. YOU'RE NOT SICK AT ALL. GO AWAY.

THINK ABOUT IT, MAUREEN. WE'VE JUST SPENT SEVERAL DAYS STRAIGHT HIKING...

WITH OUR BACKPACKS FULLY LOADED...

BLA BLA BLA BLA BLA BLA

BLA BLA

YOUR MUSCLES ARE JUST SORE, THAT'S ALL!

I'M SORE ALL OVER, TOO. WHEN YOU WORK YOUR MUSCLES FOR THAT LONG...

BLA BLA BLA BLA BLA BLA BLA

THEY GET TIGHT AND THEY HURT. NOTHING COULD BE MORE NORMAL.

BUT THEN...

WHOA, POOR ALANIS. YOUR TONGUE MUST BE SO SORE!

CAZENOVE & WILLIAM

73

YUM. WE'RE SO GOING TO ENJOY THESE FRESH HAZELNUTS, ALANIS.

YESSS... WE'VE GOT TONS OF THEM.

HEY, MAUREEN. THIS ROCK IS STRONG ENOUGH TO CRACK THEM, DON'T YOU THINK?

LET ME SEE THAT.

BONK BONK BONK

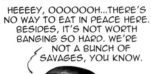

HEEEEY, OOOOOOH...THERE'S NO WAY TO EAT IN PEACE HERE. BESIDES, IT'S NOT WORTH BANGING SO HARD. WE'RE NOT A BUNCH OF SAVAGES, YOU KNOW.

OKAY! GENTLY, GENTLY...

TUNK TUNK TUNK

⸓ARRGH⸓... GIVE ME THAT!

I'M GOING TO SHOW YOU ONCE AND FOR ALL.

SWIP.

IT'S NOT EVEN ALL THAT HARD...

BRUK

OUCH!

WHY ARE YOU YELLING SO LOUD! WE'RE NOT A BUNCH OF SAVAGES, YOU KNOW.

GUFFAW!

OW! OUCH! OUCHIE! OW! OW! OW! OW! OW! OW!

CAZENOVE & WILLIAM

IT'S BEEN A LONG TIME SINCE DAD AND MOM HAVE BROUGHT US HERE, RIGHT, SISTER?!

WOO-HOO! I LOVE IT *SO MUCH!* WE'RE GOING TO HAVE AN AWESOME TIME, WENDY!

WHAT DO YOU WANT TO START WITH? I'LL LET YOU PICK.

NO RUNNING ON THE BEACH. NO DIVING. NO EATING. NO SINKING.

YOU'VE GOT THE *SLIDE OF FEAR,* WHICH LOOKS WILD...

MMM...

IF NOT THAT, YOU'VE GOT THE *WATER WARS...*

DID YOU SEE? THEY'VE EVEN GOT THE *PINK PANTHER.*

THE *CANOE RAPIDS RACE* IS NEW AND IT LOOKS TOTALLY INSANE...

SO. HAVE YOU DECIDED? WHAT DO YOU WANT TO DO?

I KNOW. I KNOW WHAT I WANT TO START WITH RIGHT HERE AND NOW!

NOOOO...I CAN'T BELIEVE IT. YOU'RE PLAYING *20 QUESTIONS* HERE?!

I'VE GIVEN UP TRYING TO UNDERSTAND HOW MY SISTER THINKS...

EMMA, YOU LOSE! YOU HAVE TO ASK A *YES* OR *NO* QUESTION. HA-HA. LOSER!

CAZENOVE & WILLIAM

IF YOU GET A CHANCE, DON'T HESITATE. GO SEE THEM IN CONCERT.

DEFINITELY! *SHAKA PONK* TOTALLY ROCKS.

WENDY...

THE WHOLE PLACE WENT CRAZY STARTING WITH THE FIRST SONG...

WENDY...

WHOA.

BUT YOU KNOW WHAT? THANKS TO MASON'S UNCLE, WE HAD BACKSTAGE ACCESS...

IT'S BACKSTAGE PASSES...

WENDY...

NOT ONLY DID WE SEE THEM, BUT WE GOT TO TALK TO THEM. *WOW!* THEY EVEN AUTOGRAPHED A *CD* AND MY CAP.

SHE HASN'T TAKEN IT OFF SINCE THEN... HA-HA!

WENDY...

AWESOME, YOU KNOW... HONESTLY, I SCREEEAMED...

ANYWAY, BEFORE THE CONCERT, I LIKED THEM OKAY, BUT NOW I'M TOTALLY CRAZY ABOUT THEM.

A TRUE FAN!

HA! HA! HA!

WENDY...

WENNNDYYY...

WHAT?!

YOU CAN WRITE THAT DOWN, ALANIS: THE OLDER YOU GET, THE DEAFER YOU GET.

WHATEVS!

TOTALLY! YOU CALLED HER AT LEAST 10 TIMES BEFORE SHE ANSWERED.

COME ON. LET'S GO TEST YOUR PARENTS NOW.

CAZENOVE & WILLIAM

I'M NOT AFRAID OF ANYTHING!

I'M A REAL DAREDEVIL.

YEEHAAAA!

GERONIMO!

WAH-HOO!

I'M FLYING!

WEEE!

SPLASH

YESSS... THAT WAS TOO TOTALLY AWESOME. I'M GOING BACK. YEHAAAH!

YOU KNOW, SAMMIE, I WOULD'VE NEVER THOUGHT I'D SAY THIS, BUT THIS TIME, I'D REALLY LIKE TO KNOW WHAT GOES ON IN MY SISTER'S HEAD.

DEFINITELY!

CAZENOVE & WILLIAM

CAZENOVE & WILLIAM

PHOOEY! YOU'RE POUTING THE WAY I DO WHEN I'VE LOST AT DODGEBALL.

YUP... I DON'T FEEL SO HOT.

MMPFF...

YOU'RE COLD? DO YOU WANT ME TO GET YOU A SWEATER?

FORGET IT! I'M WONDERING IF MASON REALLY LIKES ME. THERE.

WE LIKE TOTALLY DIFFERENT THINGS...

HE ADORES SOCCER. I THINK IT'S FOR THE BIRDS. I'M A MOVIE BUFF; HE FALLS ASLEEP.

WHEN I WANT TO TAKE A WALK IN THE WOODS, HE'D RATHER PLAY LAME GAMES ON HIS SMART-PHONE.

ETC. ETC.

AH, OKAY. IT'S LIKE THE TWO OF US, ACTUALLY.

WHAT?

WUMP WUMP WUMP

I HATE WHAT YOU WEAR.

YOU PUT ON MAKEUP THAT'S WORSE THAN STUFF FOR HALLOWEEN.

AND YOUR PERFUME STINKS LIKE SOUP.

BUT DESPITE ALL THAT, YOU'RE MY FAVORITE BIG SISTER WHO I LOVE SO MUCH.

WHAT YOU'RE SAYING MAKES SENSE.

WE DON'T HAVE TO LIKE THE SAME THINGS TO LIKE EACH OTHER.

THANKS, SIS. I'LL GO BACK AND BE WITH MY MASON...

SMEK

BUT WHEN I GET BACK, WE'RE GOING TO TALK ABOUT THIS BUSINESS OF MAKEUP, THREADS, AND PERFUME THAT STINKS LIKE SOUP.

GULP!

CAZENOVE & WILLIAM

HEY, MISS WALKING DISASTER, WE NEED TO TALK ABOUT WHAT YOU SAID THE OTHER DAY, Y'KNOW?!

AH!

TO LIFT MY SPIRITS WHEN I DIDN'T FEEL SO HOT...

YOU WOUND UP TELLING ME THAT--

HEY, ARE YOU LISTENING TO ME?!

YEAH, YEAH...

I DIDN'T LIKE IT ALL THAT MUCH WHEN YOU LET IT SLIP THAT MY PERFUME STINKS LIKE SOUP, BECAUSE, FIRST OF ALL, MASON GAVE ME THAT PERFUME.

MMM

SO YOU'D BE WELL ADVISED TO APOLOGIZE. THE SMELL OF SOUP ISN'T NICE AND IT'S--

OH, HEY!

MMM

OH, COME ON! WHAT ARE YOU--

≶SNIFF≶ ≶SNIFF≶ ≶SNIFF≶

FISH SOUP

FISH SOUP

WENDY DUMPED YOU AGAIN, RIGHT?

NO, SHE JUST TOLD ME NEVER TO GIVE HER ANY MORE PRESENTS.

CAZENOVE & WILLIAM

DODGEBALL.
DODGEBALL.

WOO-HOOOO!

COME ON,
MAUREEN.
LET'S PICK
TEAMS.

I'LL PICK
SAMMIE.

YES!

I'LL PICK...
LULU, TO BE ON
THE WINNING
TEAM.

YES!

YES!

CAMILLE'S
WITH US.

YESSS,
GOOD
CHOICE,
COUSIN.

ALANIS,
WITH ME!

EMMA,
YOU COME
OVER HERE.

NAT,
YOU'RE
WITH ME.

YIPPIE!

COME
ON, GIRLS,
WE'RE OFF!

WAIT,
WHERE'RE
YOU
GOING?

HEY! DON'T
LEAVE...

LET'S PLAY ANOTHER
ROUND...EXCEPT THIS
TIME, I'LL PICK
FIRST.

CAZENOVE & WILLIAM

SO WHO'S THIS NICE BIG CARAMEL CAKE WITH SARDINES IN OIL FOR?

FOR MY MONSTROTEDDIES, OF COURSE!

IT'S STUPID THAT MY OVEN DOESN'T REALLY HEAT, WENDY.

THANK GOODNESS! IT'S A TOY.

IT'S LIKE YOUR COFFEEMAKER. YOU NOTICED THAT IT DOESN'T MAKE REAL COFFEE, I HOPE?!

BUT...

LOOK, DO YOU REALLY THINK YOUR LASER GUN FIRES A DEATH RAY?

WEEEELL...

DITTO FOR YOU CASH REGISTER AND YOUR HORSE...

THEY'RE TOYS, MAUREEN.

IT'S NOT COMPLICATED, YOU KNOW.

TAP TAP

NOOOO...

WHEN SOMETHING'S SMALLER THAN THE REAL THING AND DOESN'T REALLY LOOK LIKE IT, THEN IT'S A *TOY!*

TAP TAP

!?

WA'AAH!

I'M NOT A *TOY...*

CAZENOVE & WILLIAM

COME ON, LET'S ZOOM TO THE SKATE PARK...

MEG AND EMMA SHOULD ALREADY BE THERE.

WAIT FOR ME. I'M COMING.

OKAY, WENDY, BUT HURRY!

LOOK, MAUREEN...

I'D LIKE TO SHOW YOU A TRICK.

FOCUS... HERE GOES.

3...

...1...

2...

TUNK TUNK TUNK

TUNK

...14...

...15...

...13...

TUNK

TUNK

CLAP CLAP

WOW! YOU ROCK!

I'VE CRUSHED YOUR RECORD OF *5* REBOUNDS...

AND WITHOUT BREAKING A SWEAT, ON TOP OF THAT.

WE'RE GOOD, GIRLS. WE'LL GET SOME PEACE...

IT'LL TAKE HER AT LEAST A WHOLE DAY...

1...2... 2 AND A HALF...

HA! HA! HA!

HA! HA! HA!

HA! HA! HA!

CAZENOVE & WILLIAM

SOMETIMES I GET THE FEELING THAT I SHARE MY LIFE WITH A WARTHOG...

YUCK!

I SHWALLOWED THE PISHA IN ONE FELL SHWOOP! DIDJA SEE?!

GULP GULP

NUM NUM NUM

OR WITH A SLOTH, A HUGE LAZYBONES...

SNORRRR
SNOOR
RRE
SNORRRR

MY SISTER'S ALSO A LITTLE LIKE A BROWN BEAR...

SOMETIMES LIKE A LION THAT'S READY TO ATTACK...

YOU! I'M GOING TO...

WELL, YES, OKAY, YES. LOL. FINISH YOUR PUDDING FIRST.

A HYENA...

ARE YOU LOOKING FOR PAPA SMURF?

HEE HEE EEH HEE EEH HEE HEE EEH

WHATEVS!

AN ORANGUTAN...

HONK HONK HONK HONK

ARGH!

SO YOU DON'T WANT TO GO TO THE ZOO WITH US?!

NO, NO, I'M FINE. I KNOW ALL ABOUT ANIMALS.

CAZENOVE & WILLIAM

OH, MY GOSH! WE HAD THE MOST INCREDIBLE VACATION, Y'KNOW, MEG...

ME TOO! I WANT TO TELL MEG.

WELL, FIRST, THE PORTNAWAK RUN. I TOTALLY ADORE THAT RACE.

ME TOO. I ADORE IT! RIGHT, WENDY?!

SLURP

THEN WE SPENT TWO DAYS IN THE SUN AT--

AT THE AQUA TICK PARK!

WE STAYED AT OUR GRANDPARENTS AND--

AND THEIR DOGGY, DARWIN, WAS WITH ME THE WHOLE TIME...

IN MY BED, UNDER MY CHAIR, AND EVEN IN THE BATHTUB, HEE-HEE.

OUR COUSINS ALANIS AND CAMILLE SPENT THE WHOLE SUMMER WITH US.

THEY'RE BOTH REALLY NICE.

BUT OF COURSE. THEY'RE OUR COUSINS.

WELL, THERE YOU GO. SCHOOL STARTS BACK UP TOMORROW. I HAVE TO GO, MEG.

YES, WE'VE GOT SO MUCH HOMEWORK. I NEED TO GO, TOO.

⸮OOF,⸮ IT'S TOUGH!

WELL, I HAVE TO GO, TOO, FOR STARTERS...

YOU'VE GOT HOME-WORK?

WELL, YES. LOADS OF IT. I NEED TO GET A TRICK READY TO PLAY ON DAD AND MOM...

I HAVE TO MAKE UP JOKES TO TELL NAT AND LULU...

I ALSO NEED TO GO POKING THROUGH YOUR ROOM...

⸮OOF!⸮ IT'S TOUGH!

CAZENOVE & WILLIAM

CAZENOVE & WILLIAM

AT SOME POINT IN THE FOREST, IT WAS SUPER FUN...

IT WAS FULL OF STUFF AND OF--

HANG ON, I'LL BE RIGHT BACK!

SO, I WAS SAYING. ALONG THE PATH, THERE WERE A BUNCH OF DEAD LEAVES, LIKE A CARPET. LOTS AND LOTS OF THEM, EVERYWHERE.

AND DIRT ON TOP OF THEM, TOO.

I CAN'T FORGET THE BIG PEBBLES! SO MANY OF THEM WERE SO INTERESTING!

BOC
BOC
BOC

CUBIK ROCKS

AND THEN?

THERE YOU HAVE IT! I'LL EXPLAIN. I WENT LIKE THAT ALONG THE PATH...

AND THEN AFTER THAT, ALL OF A SUDDEN...

...NO, COME ON. I'LL JUST TELL YOU ABOUT IT RIGHT THERE. IT'LL BE EASIER...

OH, NO! NO WAY!

YES, WAY. AND I'M SURE MAUREEN WILL FIND A GREAT EXCUSE, ON TOP OF IT... ⇒GROAN!⇐

CAZENOVE & WILLIAM

HA HA! DIDJA SEE WHAT GREEDY GUSSES THEY ARE?

HERE, CHICKIE CHICKIE CHICKIE

HEEHEE! THEY LOVE SNACKS.

UHMM, COULD SOMEONE GIVE ME SOME BREAD FOR THE SWANS? I DIDN'T BRING ANY.

WELL, THAT WAS MY LAST CRUST, MAUREEN.

HMMPH...

SAME HERE.

AND I FINISHED MY CROISSANT.

SO WHAT'RE YOU GOING TO GIVE THEM?

KRINKLE KRINKLE

ACTUALLY, I THINK THAT...

BE CAREFUL, MAUREEN...

IT'S ESPECIALLY IMPORTANT NOT TO GIVE THEM ANY CANDY, BECAUSE IT'S BAD FOR THEIR TEETH.

DON'T WORRY, ALANIS, THIS ISN'T CANDY.

HA! HA! HA!

IT'S JUST MONEY. THAT WAY THEY CAN GO BUY WHAT THEY WANT!

CAZENOVE & WILLIAM

ARGH! IT'S A DISASTER...A DISASTER. I'M GETTING MY *STARS MAG* TODAYYYY... DISAAAA--

UHH...IS IT ALL THAT BAD?

BIG TIME! IT'S RAINING CATS AND DOGS.

AH, YES. IT'S RAINING. I KNOW!

AND THIS MORNING, I PUT A SPECIAL CONDITIONER IN MY HAIR...

ABOVE ALL, I CAN'T GET IT WET, OR ELSE IT WILL BLOW UP LIKE A BALLOON AT A COUNTY FAIR!

LOL! YOU'LL HAVE HAIR LIKE A GREMLIN?!

IT'LL CHANGE COLOR...

TANGLE UP AND GET HARD AND PRICKLY.

TRAUMA ON STEROIDS!

AND THEN AFTERWARDS, I'LL HAVE TO GO TO THE HAIR DOCTOR. HE'LL SHAVE MY HEAD... IT'LL BE HORRIBLE.

MASON WILL NEVER LOOK AT ME THE SAME AGAIN.

BOO-HOO HOO HOO HOO!

I DIDN'T KNOW ALL THAT...

BOOHOO HOO HOO HOO

COME ON, STOP WHINING.

I'LL GO TO THE MAILBOX *MYSELF.*

MY HAIR ISN'T AFRAID OF ANYTHING.

HEE-HEE! LET'S HOPE SHE DOESN'T GROW UP TOO QUICKLY.

CAZENOVE & WILLIAM

WENDY, DO YOU HAVE THE BOOK ON WELL-BUILT CASTLES?

STRONG CASTLES?! YOU ALREADY CHECKED OUT BOXES OF THEM FROM THE LIBRARY YESTERDAY.

YEAH, BUT I'D LIKE TO HAVE OTHERS.

OKAY, LOOK IN MY ROOM, ON THE TOP SHELF.

OR ELSE IN MY CLOSET...

BUT DON'T MAKE A MESS!

DON'T WORRY. YOU KNOW ME.

I FOUND TWO. I'M TAKING THEM.

AND DO YOU HAVE ANY ABOUT KNIGHTS AND PEASANTS IN THE MIDDLE AGES?

Strong Castles

YES, I HAVE THOSE TOO. TAKE WHAT YOU WANT.

OKAY! I'LL TAKE ALL OF THEM. THANKS, WENDY DEAR.

I'LL BE AWHILE... ÷OOF!÷...

MAUREEN'S TEACHING HERSELF SOMETHING... HOLY COW, THAT'S CRAZY, ANYWAY...

SLURP

HEE-HEE! MY SISTER THINKS IT'S TO READ THEM...

NOOO, REALLY?

LOL! SHE'S HOPELESS!

Strong Castles

CAZENOVE & WILLIAM

COME ON, MAUREEN!

YOU'RE THE CHAMPION!

TO THINK THAT YOU DID THIS RACE WHEN YOU WERE JUST KIDS.

AH, YES. IT'S AN INSTITUTION HERE, *THE PORTNAWAK RUN.*

ANYWAY, YOUR SISTER WAS ALWAYS FULL OF BEANS.

HA! RIGHT NOW, THERE'S LOTS OF MUD, YOU KNOW.

AND MAUREEN PASSES AHEAD!

MAUREEEN'S THE WINNER!

YES!

SHE HASN'T CHANGED VERY MUCH, AS A MATTER OF FACT.

CLAP CLAP CLAP

OH, YES, SHE'S MUCH MORE MATURE THOUGH.

HUH, WHA--?!

WELL, OKAY, WENDY...

ACTUALLY, NO, SHE HASN'T CHANGED AT ALL!

SINCE WHEN DID YOU STOP CARRYING ME IN YOUR ARMS WHEN I WIN?

MWAH-HA-HA! HA! HA! HA!

CAZENOVE & WILLIAM

WATCH OUT FOR PAPERCUTZ ™

Welcome to the fighting-mad, fifth THE SISTERS "M.Y.O.B."* graphic novel, featuring our favorite ferocious females, Wendy and Maurine, by Christophe Cazenove and William Maury, from Papercutz—those innocent bystanders dedicated to publishing great graphic novels for all ages. I'm Jim Salicrup, the Editor-in-Chief and official Portnawak Run costumed mascot, and I'm here to take you behind-the-scenes at Papercutz and tell you about exciting new projects...

But first, I'd like to share a little background on the co-creator of THE SISTERS, writer Christophe Cazenove. Mr. Cazenove (not to be confused with the late actor, Christophe Cazenove) was born in the beautiful coastal town of Martigues, France, in 1969. Christophe has been a comics fan all his life, and when it came time to launch his career, his early efforts to work in the comics industry led to a twelve-year career... in supermarkets.

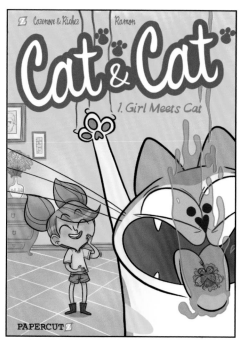

CAT & CAT © 2012, 2019 Bamboo Édition.

But Christophe never gave up on his dream of a comics career, and by the tenth year of his employment in frozen foods, one of his comics projects attracted the attention of comics writer and editor Olivier Sulpice: *Predictions of Nostra*. After that, he regularly worked for French publisher Bamboo putting his humor to work on series such as *Gendarmes, the Fire, the Driving School* and finally, THE SISTERS, which became a huge success in France. Papercutz is proud to be the English language publisher of THE SISTERS and we're proud to announce that we'll soon be publishing yet another graphic novel series written by Christophe Cazenove, this one co-written with Hervé Richez, and illustrated by the very talented Yrgane Ramon, called CAT & CAT.

Some say that we're publishing so many graphic novels with cats that perhaps we should consider changing our name to *Papercatz*. Be that as it may, CAT & CAT is about a young girl named Cat—short for Catherine—and her new pet cat, Sushi, and their life together with Cat's dad. Between turning everything into a scratching post and the constant game of "love me/leave me alone," Cat and her dad have a lot to learn about cats. To give you an even better idea of what I'm talking about, we're featuring a short preview of CAT & CAT #1 "Girl Meets Cat" on the following pages. Chances are if you've enjoyed the characters and humor of THE SISTERS, you'll also love CAT & CAT.

For those paying close attention, you'll recall that I said I was going to tell you about two exciting new projects. Well, CAT & CAT is one, so what's the other exciting new Papercutz project? Glad you asked! It's also written by the tireless Christophe Cazenove, and even illustrated by William Maury. No, it's not THE SISTERS #6 "Hurricane Maureen," which is also coming soon, I said a "new" project. It's called THE SUPER SISTERS, and it's an all-new graphic novel featuring Wendy and Maureen as the super-heroes they often imagine themselves to be! No matter how many super-hero movies you may've seen, we guarantee nothing compares to these super-powered siblings!

So, there you have it! Coming your way soon from Papercutz are three more fun graphic novels: CAT & CAT #1, THE SISTERS #6, and THE SUPER SISTERS! Look for them at your favorite booksellers or at your local library. And guess what? That's not all! There's more great graphic novels created just for you coming from Papercutz! Which is why we always say, "Watch out for Papercutz!"

Thanks,

Jim

*When I asked Editor Jeff Whitman what "M.Y.O.B." stood for, I think he wasn't in a very good mood. He just looked at me and said, "Mind Your Own Beeswax."

STAY IN TOUCH!

EMAIL:	salicrup@papercutz.com
WEB:	www.papercutz.com
TWITTER:	@papercutzgn
INSTAGRAM:	@papercutzgn
FACEBOOK:	PAPERCUTZGRAPHICNOVELS
FANMAIL:	Papercutz, 160 Broadway, Suite 700, East Wing, New York, NY 10038